NANCY

AND THE CLUE CREW®

#32

Cape Mermaid Mystery

Trouble is brewing on the Cape!

CAROLYN KEENE ILLUSTRATED BY MACKY PAMINTUAN

Crack these other cases!

ISBN 978-1-4424-4625-0
$4.99 U.S./$5.99 Can.

A Spooky Start

Nancy and her friends followed Tessie out of the room. At the end of the hallway she opened a door that led to a set of narrow, carpeted stairs. She switched on a light and also grabbed a flashlight that was hanging on the wall.

The four girls soon reached the top of the stairs. Nancy glanced around the attic, which was jam-packed with dusty furniture, old toys, and cardboard boxes. Even though the space was hot and stuffy, she couldn't help but shiver a little.

Tessie arced her flashlight this way and that. "Marshmallow Fluff? Vanilla Cream? Are you up here?" she called out.

The beam of her flashlight lit up something on the wall.

"Look!" Bess cried out, pointing.

Someone—or something—had scrawled the words *Help me* in a layer of dust.

Join the CLUE CREW & solve these other cases!

#1 *Sleepover Sleuths*

#2 *Scream for Ice Cream*

#3 *Pony Problems*

#4 *The Cinderella Ballet Mystery*

#5 *Case of the Sneaky Snowman*

#6 *The Fashion Disaster*

#7 *The Circus Scare*

#8 *Lights, Camera . . . Cats!*

#9 *The Halloween Hoax*

#10 *Ticket Trouble*

#11 *Ski School Sneak*

#12 *Valentine's Day Secret*

#13 *Chick-napped!*

#14 *The Zoo Crew*

#15 *Mall Madness*

#16 *Thanksgiving Thief*

#17 *Wedding Day Disaster*

#18 *Earth Day Escapade*

#19 *April Fool's Day*

#20 *Treasure Trouble*

#21 *Double Take*

#22 *Unicorn Uproar*

#23 *Babysitting Bandit*

#24 *Princess Mix-up Mystery*

#25 *Buggy Breakout*

#26 *Camp Creepy*

#27 *Cat Burglar Caper*

#28 *Time Thief*

#29 *Designed for Disaster*

#30 *Dance off*

#31 *Make-a-Pet Mystery*

Nancy Drew and the Clue Crew®

#32

Cape Mermaid Mystery

By Carolyn Keene

Illustrated by Macky Pamintuan

Aladdin
New York London Toronto Sydney New Delhi

ALADDIN
An imprint of Simon & Schuster Children's Publishing Division
1230 Avenue of the Americas, New York, NY 10020
First Aladdin paperback edition May 2012

Designed by Lisa Vega
The text of this book was set in ITC Stone Informal.
Manufactured in the United States of America 0312 OFF
10 9 8 7 6 5 4 3 2 1
Library of Congress Control Number 2011939421
ISBN 978-1-4424-4625-0
ISBN 978-1-4424-4626-7 (eBook)

CONTENTS

Chapter One: Spooky Noises · · · · · · · · · · · · · · 1

Chapter Two: The Ghost of Cape Mermaid · · · 12

Chapter Three: Ghostly Encounters · · · · · · · 23

Chapter Four: A Sighting · · · · · · · · · · · · · · · · · 31

Chapter Five: A Strange Clue · · · · · · · · · · · 37

Chapter Six: The Return of the Ghost · · · · 45

Chapter Seven: The Gold Coin · · · · · · · · · · · · · 52

Chapter Eight: Family Tree · · · · · · · · · · · · · · 60

Chapter Nine: An Almost Invisible Clue · · · · 66

Chapter Ten: The Competition! · · · · · · · · · · · 76

CHAPTER ONE

Spooky Noises

"I can smell the ocean!" eight-year-old Nancy Drew exclaimed as she rolled down the car window.

"I can hear seagulls!" George Fayne added excitedly.

"I can see the ice-cream stand!" George's cousin Bess Marvin piped up. "Can we stop, Mr. Drew? *Pleeeeeease?*"

"Pleeeeeease?" Nancy and George chimed in.

Laughing, Carson Drew made a right turn onto Neptune Street. "I promise we can go later. I don't want to spoil your appetites for dinner."

"Okay, Daddy," Nancy said. "Are we eating at their house? Or at a restaurant?"

"Their house is a hotel, so I'm not sure," the Drews' housekeeper, Hannah Gruen, said. She was in the passenger seat next to Carson, with a road map spread out across her lap. "There it is, on the right," she added, pointing. "Oh my gosh, it's beautiful!"

Nancy craned her neck for a better look. Ahead of them was a big Victorian mansion. It was pale blue with purple shutters, and it had a gold weather vane on top in the shape of a

mermaid. The sign in front read: MERMAID INN, 1879.

Nancy, Carson, Hannah, and Nancy's best friends, George and Bess, were visiting Carson's cousin Claire Katz. Claire and her husband, Leo, owned the inn, which was in the seaside town of Cape Mermaid, New Jersey. The Katzes had two daughters: Tessie, who was ten, and Amanda, who was six. Carson, a lawyer, was going to do some legal work for Leo and Claire. While he was busy, Nancy, George, and Bess were going to explore Cape Mermaid with Hannah. Nancy couldn't wait!

Carson pulled into the driveway and parked the car. Nancy and her friends grabbed their rolling suitcases from the back and half-ran, half-walked through the front yard. Seashells crunched under their feet on the path, which wound through a garden full of fragrant roses, honeysuckle, and lavender. Nancy could make out a pale stretch of sandy beach just beyond the backyard.

The front door burst open just before they reached it. "Yay, you're here!" a little girl said, jumping up and down. She had short, wavy brown hair, and she was wearing a polka-dot bathing suit, a pink ballet tutu, and one orange flip-flop.

"You must be Amanda," Carson said as he and Hannah caught up to everyone.

A second girl joined Amanda, dressed in a white beach cover-up. She was taller, with shoulder-length, dark blond hair. It was hard to see her face, though, because she was holding a small purple video camera in front of it. A little red light was flashing, which meant that it was in record mode.

Carson bent down and waved awkwardly at the camera. "Uh, hi. You must be Tessie."

"Hi, Carson! Hi, Carson's friends and family!" Tessie slowly panned her camera from left to right. "This is Tessie Katz, reporting from Cape Mermaid," she said in a serious-sounding voice. "These people have just arrived at the

Mermaid Inn after a long drive from River Heights, Illinois. What will they find here in Cape Mermaid? A relaxing summer vacation? An exciting adventure? Or something else? Stay tuned!"

George pointed to the camera. "Is that the brand-new KidCam? I've been saving up my allowance to buy one!"

Tessie lowered the camera from her face. "It's supercool! It records video digitally onto a memory card."

"I would have no idea how to work one of those," Hannah joked to Carson.

"Me neither. Kids these days are way smarter about technology than we are," Carson agreed. He turned to Tessie and Amanda. "Are your parents here? They're expecting us."

"They're in the kitchen, making spaghetti and meatballs! That's my favorite, favorite food!" Amanda exclaimed. "Come on!"

Nancy and the others followed the two sisters inside and down a long hallway. The inside of the inn was as beautiful as the outside, with pale blue walls, white wicker furniture, and vases of fresh flowers. A couple of cats were sitting on a windowsill, grooming themselves.

In the kitchen at the end of the hall, Claire was standing at the stove, stirring sauce in a large pot. Leo was at the sink, chopping vegetables. Nancy didn't remember them except from photos. Nancy's parents had brought her to Cape Mermaid when she was just a baby. Her mom had died when she was three years old, and Hannah had helped take care of her ever since.

"You're here! Hello!" Claire turned off the burner and rushed over to give Carson a hug. She turned to Nancy and gave her a hug too. "Wow, you've gotten so big since the last time I saw you!"

Carson introduced everyone. "George and Bess are cousins. They're in the same class as Nancy," he finished.

"Carson, didn't you mention in an e-mail

once that these girls are detectives?" Leo asked with a wink.

"Detectives? What kind of detectives?" Tessie asked curiously.

"We have a club called the Clue Crew, and we solve mysteries," Bess replied.

"Really?" Tessie's blue eyes lit up. "What kind of mysteries?"

"All kinds of mysteries. Once, we figured out who took a bunch of newborn chicks from our classroom. And another time we found a supervaluable pet bug that was missing," Nancy explained.

"Bugs? *Ew!*" Amanda said, making a face.

Claire went back to the stove. "I'm sure you're all hungry after your long trip. Tessie, are Michaela and Emma joining us for dinner? If so, tell them to be over in ten minutes. Leo, can you show our guests up to their rooms? I can finish up the salads." She added, "We'll be eating in our family dining room across the hall. We don't have a restaurant here."

"What can we do to help?" Carson asked.

"Nothing at all. Let me show you your rooms, then we can come back down for Claire's famous spaghetti and meatballs," Leo said cheerfully.

"You guys are going to *love* Cape Mermaid. There's so much to do here!" Michaela said.

"Yeah, like whale-watching. And shopping. And eating tons and tons of candy at the Candygram Shoppe," Emma added.

Michaela and Emma were Tessie's two best friends from school. Michaela had a habit of twirling her long, pale blond hair. Emma wore a red baseball cap over her curly brown hair.

Dinner was over. Michaela, Emma, and Tessie were hanging out with Nancy, George, and Bess in their room while they unpacked. Nancy loved the room, which had rose-print wallpaper and big windows that overlooked the ocean. There was an antique bookshelf with a bunch of kids' books, seashells, and a small marble mermaid statuette.

Tessie was sitting cross-legged on the floor and peering through the viewfinder of her video camera. "I got lots of cool footage today," she remarked. "Hey, Clue Crew! Maybe I could interview you guys sometime about all the mysteries you've solved?"

"Sure. Are you making a movie or something?" Nancy asked.

"Actually, we're—" Michaela began.

"I just like to shoot a bunch of random stuff," Tessie cut in. She stared pointedly at Michaela and Emma. "Don't you guys have to be home by now? It's eight." She tapped on her watch.

Michaela and Emma exchanged a glance, then jumped to their feet. "Oh, yeah! It's late! Bye!" Emma said, waving.

"Maybe we can all do something tomorrow," Michaela suggested, grabbing her ballet bag.

Bess nodded. "Definitely!"

The two girls took off. As Nancy, Bess, and George finished putting their clothes away, Tessie told them about more fun things to do in town.

"There's the boardwalk, the ice-cream stand, and, oh yeah, the beach!" Tessie went on. "There's the history museum too. The lady who runs it, Mrs. Bishop, is kind of cranky, though."

Nancy was about to reply when she heard weird noises upstairs. It sounded like a soft crash, then footsteps, then something being dragged across the floor.

The other girls heard it too. "What *is* that?" George whispered to Tessie.

Tessie frowned. "I'm not sure. Maybe one of the cats is stuck in the attic. We'd better go check it out!"

Nancy and her friends followed Tessie out of the room. At the end of the hallway, she opened a door that led to a set of narrow, carpeted stairs. She switched on a light and also grabbed a flashlight that was hanging on the wall.

The girls soon reached the top of the stairs. Nancy glanced around the attic, which was jam-packed with dusty furniture, old toys, and cardboard boxes. Even though the space was hot and stuffy, she couldn't help but shiver a little.

Tessie arced her flashlight this way and that. "Marshmallow Fluff? Vanilla Cream? Are you up here?" she called out.

The beam of her flashlight lit up something on the wall.

"Look!" Bess cried out, pointing.

Someone—or something—had scrawled the words *HELP ME* in a layer of dust.

CHAPTER TWO

The Ghost of Cape Mermaid

"The ghost was here!" Tessie burst out.

"Ghost? What ghost?" George demanded.

Tessie peered around nervously. "I wasn't going to tell you guys," she whispered. "But Cape Mermaid is haunted by a ghost. The ghost of Rowena Ellison!"

Nancy peered around too. The four of them *seemed* to be the only ones in the attic, human or otherwise. "Who's Rowena Ellison?" she asked Tessie.

"She was an artist, and she was born in Cape Mermaid, like, a hundred years ago," Tessie explained. "People have seen her—I mean, her *ghost*—around town. And she's left weird, spooky messages, too, like this one. Michaela and Emma and I are videotaping everything we can about her. Hey, I'd better videotape this, too!" She clicked on her KidCam and swiveled it toward the words on the wall.

"*Welllllll* . . . I'm not a big fan of ghosts, so maybe I should just wait down in our room for you guys," Bess said, heading for the stairs.

"Bess, wait!" Nancy walked up to the wall and peered closely at the message. It was written in block letters. She noted that the letter *H* in *HELP* was kind of smudged.

Nancy turned to Tessie. "Maybe someone wrote this message as a joke. Does your family use this attic a lot? Are your guests allowed to come up here?"

Tessie shrugged. "No, the guests aren't allowed. And we really don't use this attic much. I mean, my parents keep stuff up here, but they usually only come up here, like, twice a year—right before summer to get summer stuff, and right before the holidays to get Hanukah and Christmas stuff." She added, "I was up here after lunch today, for, like, a minute, to get my boogie board. This message wasn't there then."

"W-what if Rowena's ghost is still up here?" Bess stammered.

"There are no ghosts up here," Nancy reassured Bess. "There's no one here but us." Still, she wondered about the creepy noises they'd heard a few minutes ago. Had someone been up here? Just then, Nancy spotted a second door

on the other end of the attic. "Tessie, where does that go to?" she said curiously.

"What? Oh, um, those are stairs too. They go down to the second floor, to the laundry room, and then down to the first floor, to the kitchen," Tessie replied.

Nancy considered this. Someone could have been up here before, then escaped down the stairs to the kitchen.

And that same someone could have written the spooky message.

"Hey, I have an idea!" Tessie said suddenly. "Why don't you guys solve the mystery of Rowena's ghost? You said you're detectives, right?"

George nodded. "Right."

"You could try to figure out why she's haunting Cape Mermaid! Wouldn't that be an awesome mystery to solve?" Tessie said excitedly.

Nancy, George, and Bess looked at one another. Nancy wondered why Tessie was so eager to have the Clue Crew get on the case. But Nancy was never one to say no to a mystery. "We'll do it," Nancy said after a moment as George and Bess nodded in agreement. "But we should probably figure out if the ghost is real, first."

"Yeah. Ghosts don't exist," George added.

"Or *do* they?" Bess said, shuddering.

"Tomorrow I'll show you the video I have on my computer of the ghost. And Michaela, Emma, and I could take you for a 'ghost tour' of Cape Mermaid. *Then* maybe you guys will believe me!" Tessie insisted.

Downtown Cape Mermaid looked like something out of an old-fashioned postcard, with a boardwalk lined with quaint shops and restaurants. Just beyond, the ocean was dotted with fishing boats. Gulls and terns and other seabirds dove through the air and into the surf, searching for breakfast. The smells of the sea mingled with those of taffy and popcorn.

"We can start our ghost tour at the history

museum," Tessie told Nancy, George, Bess, and Hannah. "There's a Rowena exhibit there."

"Yeah, she was kind of famous," Michaela added.

Bess frowned. "Famous . . . for being a ghost?"

"For being an artist," Emma replied, adjusting the baseball cap on her head.

"I don't know about this ghost tour business," Hannah said worriedly. "Nancy, are you sure the Clue Crew should be getting involved in ghost-hunting?"

"We don't think there *is* a ghost, Hannah," Nancy told her.

"Of course there's a ghost! You saw her on my computer this morning!" Tessie declared.

Just after breakfast, Tessie had shown Nancy, George, and Bess a short video she took of the "ghost" two weeks ago, just outside the old, now-abandoned beach cottage Rowena used to use as an artist's studio. Nancy had to admit that the image—of a shimmery white form hovering just outside the cottage—*did* look pretty ghostly.

Still, Nancy felt that there had to be a *human* explanation. Last night she, George, and Bess had checked out the second set of stairs leading down from the attic. The stairs were carpeted, which meant that if someone had used them to escape downstairs, their footsteps would have been muffled and hard to hear.

Nancy had also learned from Claire and Leo that there was no one in the kitchen—or anywhere on the first floor—at that time, which meant that the person could have left the house unseen. The Katzes apparently kept the front and back doors unlocked until ten p.m.

Nancy and her group finally arrived at the history museum. Tucked between an antique store and a bakery called Muffin Madness, it was housed in a small brick building with plum shutters and a sign that said CAPE MERMAID HISTORY MUSEUM in big gold letters.

They all went inside. Nancy glanced around.

The front lobby was filled with black-and-white photographs of Cape Mermaid, mermaid statues, and model ships in glass cases, among other things.

There was a young man at the front desk. The name tag on his Cape Mermaid T-shirt said "Brandon." "Admission is free, so just go right on in," he said pleasantly. "You might be interested in the special exhibit on the history of whaling."

"Thanks! We're here to see the exhibit on Rowena Ellison, though," Nancy explained.

"Yeah, that exhibit's been especially popular lately. It's in the Coral Room, to your right," Brandon said.

Nancy and the others headed into the Coral Room. The Rowena Ellison exhibit took up one wall. There were various photographs of her at different stages of her life—from when she was a baby all the way to when she was a grandmother. There was also a photograph of her old beach cottage, which Nancy recognized from Tessie's video footage.

There was a big plaque with some details about her life. It said that she was born in Cape Mermaid, where she lived all her life except for a brief period when she attended art school in Philadelphia. It also said that she especially liked to paint seascapes and other local scenery, although she was often hired to paint portraits as well. She was married to an architect and had three children and six grandchildren. She died at the age of eighty-two.

There were four paintings on the wall: two seascapes, a portrait of a young girl, and one boardwalk scene. Nancy didn't know a lot about art, but she thought the paintings were really good. Rowena Ellison seemed to like playing around with colors. She used surprising, unexpected shades, like a single brushstroke of bright orange in an ocean wave.

"Please let me know if you have any questions," someone called out.

Nancy turned around. A woman was

standing in the doorways holding a clipboard. She wore gray slacks and a white cotton sweater, and her silvery hair was pulled back in a loose ponytail. Her name tag read: MRS. BISHOP. Nancy remembered Tessie saying that she was the director of the museum.

"Oh, hi, Mrs. Bishop! *I* have a question!" Tessie clicked on her KidCam and pointed it at her. "Can you tell us if you've seen the ghost of Rowena Ellison around the museum?"

she said in her serious-sounding reporter voice.

Mrs. Bishop's face turned bright red. "Don't you and your friends have better things to do than stir up trouble?" she demanded angrily.

Chapter Three

Ghostly Encounters

Tessie's face turned bright red too. "We are *not* stirring up trouble!" she said huffily. "We have proof that Rowena's ghost is haunting Cape Mermaid! She's been terrifying local citizens!"

"Yes, well, I don't have time for you little kids and your make-believe games. Excuse me." Mrs. Bishop turned on her heels and left the room.

Michaela gasped. "Seriously? Did she just call us little kids?"

"Yeah, doesn't she know we're ten? We're practically teenagers!" Emma added.

"I don't know about that," Hannah said, chuckling. "I don't think she liked the camera too much—and I do know that we should all be careful what we say to people about this so-called ghost. Maybe Mrs. Bishop is afraid that visitors will stay away from the history museum if they think it's haunted."

"Or maybe twice as many visitors will come here *because* it's haunted," Tessie said. "Ghosts are supercool!"

"More like superterrifying," Bess muttered under her breath.

As Nancy listened to the discussion, she wondered about Mrs. Bishop. Why did she get so mad when Tessie brought up the ghost? Tessie had mentioned before that Mrs. Bishop was kind of cranky. Was she just being cranky now? Or was it something else?

"Yes, I have personally encountered the ghost of Rowena Ellison," Mrs. Yamada said dramatically. The librarian put the back of her hand on her forehead and fluttered her eyelids, as though she was about to faint. "I have many stories to share! Is your video camera on?" she asked Tessie, who nodded from behind her KidCam.

"Shhhh!" several people whispered from nearby tables.

"Oh my goodness, I'm sorry! I just get so carried away on this subject that I forget we're in a library! Please, let us continue this very important conversation in my office," Mrs. Yamada said in a low voice to Tessie and the others.

Tessie, Nancy, George, Bess, Hannah, Michaela, and Emma had stopped by the Cape Mermaid Public Library as part of the "ghost tour," to interview Mrs. Yamada and also to check out a biography of Rowena Ellison. Nancy thought it was kind of funny that the patrons were reminding the librarian to be quiet, and not the other way around.

Nancy had flipped quickly through the Rowena Ellison book. In the "Family Tree" section in back, she saw that Rowena had three daughters, who eventually married and had children of their own. One of the daughters even named her own daughter Rowena.

They all followed Mrs. Yamada out of the main reading room and down the hall into her office. "So, Mrs. Yamada. Tell us about the ghost," Tessie said once they were settled. "You said you saw her, right?"

"Several times," Mrs. Yamada said. "Oh my goodness, where do I begin? Last Wednesday I was closing up here, alone, when I heard a terrifying ghostly noise. It sounded like a fierce wind whistling through tree branches!"

"Well . . . could it have *been* a fierce wind blowing through tree branches?" George asked her.

"Yeah. Wasn't last Wednesday that big storm?" Emma added.

Tessie glared at Emma. "I think we should let Mrs. Yamada talk, don't you? Go on, Mrs. Yamada," she prompted her.

Mrs. Yamada sniffed. "Yes, well, I'm one hundred percent sure it was the ghost of

Rowena Ellison! And then, on Friday, I felt a cold hand on the back of my shoulder. When I turned around, there was no one there!"

"Maybe somebody with cold hands brushed up against you by accident? And they were gone by the time you turned around?" Nancy pointed out.

"Absolutely not! It was a supernatural presence, I assure you!" Mrs. Yamada insisted. "And then there was the time several weeks ago when I saw a mysterious message scribbled on the ladies' room wall. It said, and I quote, 'Nora W. was here.'" She paused. "Don't you all get it? 'Nora W.' is an anagram of Rowena!"

Nancy knew about

anagrams from school. They were words that shared the same letters, except scrambled around.

"N, o, r, a, w . . . no, it's not," Michaela said, twirling a lock of her hair. "You're missing an *E*. Plus, I bet that was Nora Waxman. She got in big, fat trouble once for writing her name all over the girls' bathroom at school."

"Michaela!" Tessie said irritably. "Why are you and Emma being so lame? Reporters aren't supposed tell their sources they're wrong!"

"Uh, sorry," Emma grumbled. She crumpled her baseball cap in her hands.

Mrs. Yamada spent the next half hour elaborating on her stories. As Nancy listened, she began to think that maybe, just maybe, the librarian might be exaggerating a little about these "ghostly encounters." In any case, they didn't sound very ghostly to her.

"This is the perfect place to talk about our mystery!" Bess said eagerly. She sat back in the pink vinyl booth and broke off a piece of chocolate-pecan bark. "Who wants some?"

The group had stopped by the Candygram Shoppe, just around the corner from the library. George, Tessie, Michaela, and Emma all raised their hands. Hannah was up at the counter paying for everyone's candy. As the other girls chatted, Nancy searched through her backpack. With a frown she realized that she had forgotten to bring her special detective notebook from home. She always recorded the details of the Clue Crew's cases in it, such as clues and suspects.

"Does anyone have some paper and a pen I could use?" Nancy asked. "I think I left my detective notebook back in River Heights."

"Here!" Michaela reached into her bag and pulled out a slender notebook. She leafed through it quickly and tore out several pages, which she folded and put back in her backpack. Then she handed the notebook to Nancy, along with a pen. "You can keep them."

Nancy glanced at the cover of the notebook. It had a picture of a mermaid on it. "Thanks, Michaela. Are you sure?"

"Sure! I have more at home," Michaela replied.

"Great! I want to start writing down everything we've learned about Rowena's, um, ghost," Nancy said. "Let's start with clues."

Nancy opened the notebook to a clean page. Just then, she felt a cold, clammy hand on her bare shoulder. *"I . . . am . . . Rowena's . . . ghost,"* said an eerie voice.

CHAPTER FOUR

A Sighting

Nancy whirled around. Two boys were standing behind her, cracking up.

"Julio! Henry! Not funny," Tessie fumed.

One of the boys had short black hair. The other boy had sun-streaked blond hair and freckles. They were wearing T-shirts, bathing suits, and flip-flops.

"Julio did it," the blond boy said, munching on a long red licorice string.

"It was Henry's idea. He said I should stick my hand in this and prank you guys." Julio held up a cup of crushed ice.

"We heard you talking about what's-her-name's ghost," Henry went on.

"Well, you were eavesdropping. Cut it out, or I'm totally telling your parents!" Tessie said angrily.

Julio grinned. "Go ahead. They'll think you're crazy for believing in ghosts!"

After they left, Tessie sighed loudly. "They are *so* immature," she muttered under her breath.

"Julio's in my ballet class. He's a really awesome dancer," Michaela volunteered.

"And Henry's supergood at soccer," Emma added. "Hey, speaking of soccer . . . my parents just bought me the coolest new cleats. They're purple with pink stripes!"

"No way, really?" Michaela said eagerly.

Tessie rolled her eyes. "Girls! *Focus!* Otherwise we're never going to solve this case!"

Nancy picked up Michaela's pen and opened the mermaid notebook to the first page. "Tessie's right. Come on, everyone . . . let's get to work," she said.

"I love the beach!" George said, dipping her toes in the surf.

"Me too!" Tessie said.

"Me three!" Tessie's little sister Amanda added. She dug her plastic shovel into the sand. "Who wants to build a sandcastle with me?"

Hannah had brought Nancy, George, Bess, Tessie, and Amanda to Ducksbill Beach, near the Mermaid Inn. Even though it was after four o'clock, it was still hot outside, and the beach was supercrowded.

"I'll build a sandcastle with you in a minute," Nancy told Amanda as she began leafing through the mermaid notebook. "As soon as we finish going over these clues and suspects one more time."

Amanda made a face. "Clues and specks? What are those?"

"The girls are busy with their ghost mystery. Come on, Amanda, I'll build a sandcastle with you," Hannah offered. "How about over there, by those big rocks?"

"Yay!" Amanda said excitedly.

Hannah and Amanda wandered off with a big bucket of beach toys. Nancy sat up on the blanket and turned to Tessie, George, and Bess. Tessie had her KidCam on the ON position, recording the conversation.

"Okay. So here are the clues we wrote down at the candy shop earlier. There's the writing on the attic wall, plus the spooky noises, plus your video from two weeks ago, Tessie, " Nancy said, trailing her finger down the clues page. "Oh, and I wrote down everything Mrs. Yamada told us too."

"I'm not sure Mrs. Yamada really saw a ghost, though," George said. "Her stories were kind of weird."

"I know what you mean," Nancy agreed.

"Well, *I* think she definitely saw a ghost!" Tessie said firmly.

Bess held up her hand. "Me too!"

"Okay, well . . . moving on." Nancy flipped to the next page, which was the suspects page. "We haven't listed any suspects yet. What about those boys, Julio and Henry? Do you think they might be running around Cape Mermaid pretending to be Rowena's ghost?" The girls had passed Julio and Henry leaving the beach about twenty minutes ago.

Tessie peered out from behind her KidCam. "No! Besides, why do we need a list of suspects? There can't be any suspects in this case, because the ghost is real!"

"Tessie! You guys! Oh my gosh!"

Nancy looked up. Emma and Michaela were running through the sand toward them. They stopped at the edge of the beach blanket, breathless, looking really upset.

"What's wrong?" Tessie demanded.

"We . . . Michaela, you tell them!" Emma stammered.

"You'll never believe it. We just saw Rowena's ghost!" Michaela blurted out.

CHAPTER FIVE

A Strange Clue

Tessie looked confused. "Y-you saw Rowena's ghost? Where?"

"At her cottage, just now," Michaela said, pointing toward the other end of the beach. "After we left you guys at the Candygram Shoppe, I had a ballet class, and Emma had baseball practice. Then we met up at my house, and I was like, 'It's hot, do you want to go swimming?' And Emma was like, 'I don't know, do you?' And—"

"Get to the ghost part!" Tessie said impatiently. She held up her KidCam and began recording the conversation.

"Okay, okay!" Michaela said. "So we decided

to come here, and we took the shortcut that goes past Rowena's cottage. We were walking by when we saw her face in a window!"

"She was *so* scary-looking!" Emma added, shivering. Next to her, Bess shivered too.

"What did she look like?" Nancy asked the girls curiously.

Emma and Michaela exchanged a glance. "You know . . . like a ghost," Emma said after a moment.

"Yeah. She was wearing white, and she had long, wispy, spooky hair." Michaela paused. "She was staring right at us. Maybe she was trying to warn us!"

"Warn you about what?" George asked.

"To stop looking for her," Emma said in a low voice. Michaela nodded in agreement.

Nancy thought for a moment. "Did she look the same as that other time?" she said finally.

Michaela frowned. "What other time?"

"You know . . . when you guys saw her at Rowena's cottage two weeks ago?" Nancy reminded her. "Tessie showed George and Bess and me the video this morning."

"Oh, *that* time." Emma dropped her gaze and shrugged. "I guess she looked the same, yeah."

"She looked way scarier this time," Michaela added.

"Why don't we all go over to the cottage right now?" George suggested. "Maybe the ghost or whatever is still there."

"Good idea!" Nancy said.

"*Bad* idea," Bess said immediately. "You guys go along without me. I can just stay here and, uh, guard our stuff."

Nancy tugged on Bess's hand, laughing. "Come on. I promise we'll be safe. Besides, this is our big chance. Maybe we'll find out the *real* story behind our ghost!"

"Why are we visiting some dumb old house?" Amanda complained, dragging her feet on the path. "Miss Hannah and I aren't done with our princess sandcastle yet!"

"It'll be superquick and then we can go right back to the beach," Nancy promised her.

"Yeah, Amanda, and if you keep whining, I'm telling mom and dad!" Tessie threatened her sister.

"I *hate* you!" Amanda cried out.

"I hate you *more*!" Tessie shot back.

"Amanda, Tessie, let's calm down," Hannah interjected. "Nancy . . . girls . . . I want to emphasize again that we absolutely can't go inside this cottage. Even if it's abandoned, it belongs to *somebody*. Which means that we can't trespass."

"We know, Hannah," George said, nodding. "We'll be supercareful and stay outside the whole time."

"*Way* outside," Bess said emphatically.

Nancy continued leading the way down the sandy path, which wound through gentle, sloping dunes and scraggly beach plum bushes. She glanced over her shoulder at Ducksbill Beach in the distance.

She noticed that Tessie had dropped behind George, Bess, Hannah, and Amanda and joined Michaela and Emma in the rear. The three friends were whispering with their heads huddled together. Nancy wondered what they were talking about.

The group soon reached Rowena's cottage. Nancy recognized it from the photograph they'd seen that morning at the history museum, and also from Tessie's video. The cottage was small and box-shaped, with brown cedar shingles and sea-green shutters. The brown shingles were weathered and faded, and the paint on the shutters was badly chipped.

Nancy made her way to the front stoop through an overgrown garden of weeds and wildflowers. She saw that there were two windows in front of the cottage, both caked with salt and dirt and splintered with cracks.

"She was looking at us through *that* one." Michaela caught up to Nancy and pointed to the window on the right. She began twirling her hair nervously.

Nancy went up the window and peered through it. Inside was a small living room with furniture covered with light-colored sheets. Just beyond the living room was a tiny kitchen. Everything seemed incredibly dusty and cobwebby. Nancy tried to make out footprints on the floors, but it was too hard to see.

"Is she still in there?" Emma said worriedly. "Because if she is, I think we should, like, *go*."

Nancy shook her head. "No ghosts. No humans, either."

After a moment Nancy began circling around to the back of the cottage. The others followed, with Tessie videotaping the whole time. There were a couple of smaller windows that Nancy peered through too. But she couldn't see anything interesting through those, either.

She sighed in frustration. Whatever ghost or pretend ghost Michaela and Emma had seen before had disappeared.

"Can we go now? Puh-leeease? I'm soooooo bored!" Amanda begged when they'd reached the front of the cottage again.

Bess nodded. "I agree with Amanda. There's nothing here. I say we go back to the beach and build us some sandcastles!"

Nancy was about to reply when something caught her eye. A beam of sun lit up a small, metal object on the ground near the doorway.

She reached down to pick it up, brushing sand off of it. At first it looked like a gold dollar.

But after taking a closer look, Nancy could see that it wasn't a gold dollar at all. She turned it over in her hand. It looked old and tarnished. On one side was a picture of a mermaid. On the other side was a picture of a bus. Or was it a train?

Nancy's heart began racing. Could this be a clue to the ghost? Or rather, a clue to the person who was *pretending* to be the ghost?

Chapter Six

The Return of the Ghost

"Is this the nacho-cheese-flavored popcorn or the chili-spice-flavored popcorn?" Nancy asked.

Bess peeked into the bowl. "That's the nacho cheese. Try it, it's yummy!"

Nancy, Bess, and George were having a sleepover in their room at the Mermaid Inn with Tessie, Michaela, and Emma. The floor was covered with sleeping bags, pillows, backpacks, teddy bears, and yummy treats. The two cats, Marshmallow Fluff and Vanilla Cream, were curled up on one of the twin beds.

Nancy was wearing her new favorite pajamas, which were sky blue with pink heart-shaped buttons. She grabbed a handful of the nacho-cheese-flavored popcorn and opened her mermaid notebook—the one Michaela had given her.

"So now we have a new clue to add to our clues list," Nancy said out loud. "The gold coin."

Tessie turned on her KidCam. "What do we think it is?" she asked the group.

George looked thoughtful. "Well . . . it's probably not money, since it doesn't have a number on it. You know, like 'one dollar' or 'fifty cents' or whatever."

"I think it's pirate treasure!" Michaela said, grinning. "It probably came from a chest full of coins and jewels and stuff."

"Yeah. Maybe it's supervaluable," Emma agreed.

"Hmm. Maybe Rowena's ghost is hiding a big stash of pirate treasure somewhere. Or maybe she left it for us, as a message," Tessie guessed.

"What kind of message?" Bess asked her.

"I don't know. It's another piece of the mystery!" Tessie said. "And . . . *cut*! I need to take a popcorn break!"

She set her KidCam down and reached for one of the bowls.

Nancy wrote down some notes about the gold coin on the clues page. "I wonder if Julio and Henry could have dropped the coin by accident?" she mused. "They left the beach about the same time we got there. So they would have had enough time to get to Rowena's cottage. They could have gone inside and pretended to be her when you guys were walking by," she added, turning to Michaela and Emma.

"No way," Michaela said, shaking her head. "The ghost was definitely real, and she was definitely a girl—I mean, a woman. She had long hair!"

"Julio or Henry could have been wearing a wig," George said, giggling.

Nancy giggled too. "Ha-ha, funny!"

Tessie frowned. "You guys just don't get it! We're dealing with a real ghost, not a person! Besides, there's no way Julio and Henry could have been in the attic last night, pretending

to be a ghost and leaving that message on the wall!"

"Hmm. That's true," Nancy agreed.

The door swung open with a long, slow *creeeeeeak.*

Bess gave a little shriek. "Who's there?" she demanded.

Amanda hopped into the doorway. She was dressed in green dinosaur pajamas, and she was dragging a yellow sleeping bag behind her. Nancy wondered how long she had been standing there, and what she'd overheard.

"I'm ready for the sleepover!" Amanda announced cheerfully.

"Amanda, you're not invited to the sleepover. It's just for the big girls," Tessie snapped.

Amanda pouted. "But I *am* a big girl!"

There were footsteps in the hall, then Claire entered the room. "I'm sorry, girls. Amanda, sweetheart, come with me. You and I can have our own sleepover!"

"But, Mommy, I want to have a sleepover with the big girls! They're telling ghost stories!" Amanda insisted.

"Oooh, spooky! I can read you a ghost story in your bed, okay? Come on, honey." Claire took Amanda by the hand and led her away.

"It's not *faaaair*!" Nancy heard Amanda cry out.

"Sorry about my sister. She's just a baby," Tessie apologized to everyone. "Okay, so, where were we?"

The girls continued to discuss the case for a while. Michaela and Emma painted each other's toenails glittery purple. Hannah came up with more snacks: cookies, cut-up watermelon, and mugs of hot chocolate. It was almost eleven o'clock when no one could keep their eyes open anymore. They arranged their sleeping bags side by side on the floor and promptly fell asleep.

With a start, Nancy sat up in her sleeping bag. She glanced at the clock on the nightstand: 12:12 a.m.

Nearby, Bess and George were fast asleep. So were Michaela and Emma. Tessie seemed to be stirring a little, though.

Bump . . . bump . . . bump . . .

Nancy gazed up at the ceiling. The noises were coming from the attic.

Bump . . . bump . . . bump . . .

"Nancy?" Tessie whispered from her sleeping bag. "Did you hear that?"

"Yes, did you?" Nancy whispered back.

Tessie nodded. "It's the ghost. She's back!"

Chapter Seven

The Gold Coin

Something was making noises up in the attic. Nancy didn't think it was a ghost. But it definitely sounded creepy.

Nancy gestured for Tessie to follow her. The two of them stood up and tiptoed out of the room, leaving the other four girls asleep in their sleeping bags. They rushed down the hall to the door leading up to the attic. Once there, Tessie grabbed the flashlight from its hook and clicked it on.

"Shhhh," Tessie said, putting her finger on her lips. "We don't want to scare the ghost away."

Nancy nodded and gave Tessie a thumbs-up

sign. Someone was up there, ghost or no ghost.

Tessie led the way up the stairs. The weird noises continued overhead: *Bump . . . bump . . . bump.*

Nancy's heart was racing. Who—or what—was making that sound?

At the top of the stairs Tessie handed Nancy the flashlight and clicked on her KidCam, which she'd had tucked under her arm. "Who's there?" Tessie demanded.

Someone giggled. A very familiar someone.

Tessie gasped. "Amanda? Is that you?" she called out.

Amanda jumped out from behind a cardboard box.

"Boo!" she cried out. "Were you scared? Was I so, so superscary?" She bounced a big orange ball on the floor. So *that* was what was making the sound.

Nancy and Tessie exchanged a glance. "How long have you been up here?" Nancy asked Amanda.

Amanda shrugged and plucked a dust bunny from her pajamas. "I don't know. I couldn't sleep." She giggled again.

"This isn't funny, and you are in *such* big trouble," Tessie scolded her.

Nancy thought for a moment. "Amanda, were you up here last night? Pretending to be the ghost, I mean? And did you write 'Help me' on the wall?"

Nancy started to point to the message on the wall. But she realized with a start that it was gone. There was a big smudge mark where it used to be, as though someone had wiped it away. *When did that happen?* she wondered.

Nancy heard footsteps coming up the stairs. A moment later Claire and Leo appeared.

"What on earth are you girls doing up here?" Claire said, surprised.

"It's after midnight," Leo added.

"Mommy, Amanda was up here pretending to be a ghost, and it woke Nancy and me up," Tessie blurted out. "Can you give her a time-out, like, right now?"

"I don't *want* a time out!" Amanda protested. "It's not fair, because the big girls are having a sleepover, and they're solving a ghost mystery, and I'm not invited because they said I'm not a big girl! But I *am* a big girl! I'm six and a half!"

Claire and Leo exchanged a glance. "What ghost mystery?" Claire asked Tessie.

"Oh, it's nothing! We're just making up spooky-scary ghost stories, you know, ha-ha!" Tessie said quickly.

"Okay, well . . . we'll talk about this in the morning. Right now everyone needs to go back to bed," Leo said firmly.

As they all headed down the stairs, Nancy wondered: Why didn't Tessie want her parents to know about their search for Rowena's ghost?

"Mmm, I love blueberry pancakes!" George said, digging in.

"Me too." Bess turned to Nancy and Hannah. "Do you guys want a bite? How are your banana-walnut pancakes?"

"Almost as yummy as my dad's!" Nancy said with a grin. Hannah laughed and nodded.

It was Wednesday morning, and the four of them were having breakfast at a restaurant called the Seashell Café. The tables were painted different bright colors and decorated with seashells. Carson was back at the

Mermaid Inn working, and Tessie and Amanda were at their violin lessons.

Nancy took a sip of her orange juice. Then she opened up her mermaid notebook to the suspects page and picked up a pen. "So I think we should add Amanda to the suspect list," she said, writing. She had already told George and Bess about last night's incident—and Hannah, too. "That means we have three suspects now: Amanda, Julio, and Henry," she added.

Bess craned her neck to peer at the notebook. "But there's no way Amanda could have written that message on the wall," she pointed out. "It was in very neat letters. She's way too young to write that nice. I mean, my writing's really bad, and I'm, like, two years older than her."

"Plus, there's no way Amanda could have been at Rowena's cottage yesterday, scaring Michaela and Emma. She was with us on the beach," George said.

Nancy sighed and tapped her pen on the table. "I know. Amanda isn't a perfect suspect. Neither is Julio or Henry. None of our suspects is perfect."

"That's because our suspect or whatever is a ghost," Bess insisted. "You guys need to stop thinking there are real people involved!"

"I still vote for 'real people,'" George said, raising her hand.

"Me too. But which ones? We need to think of more suspects," Nancy said.

She flipped the notebook to the clues page. She had written down:

- Spooky noises coming from the attic (Monday night). And the words "Help me" written on the wall in block letters. (But then someone erased the message! Who? When?)
- Tessie's video (from two weeks before we got to Cape Mermaid).
- The funny-looking gold coin.
- PLUS Mrs. Yamada (the librarian) thinks the ghost was in the library a bunch of times.
- PLUS Michaela and Emma told us they saw

the ghost inside Rowena's cottage while we were all at the beach (Tuesday).

Hannah got up to go pay the check. Nancy's gaze fell on the line about the gold coin.

She reached into her backpack and pulled out the coin. It was stored inside a small plastic bag. The Clue Crew members often kept their clues in small plastic bags to keep them safe.

"I wish we could figure out what this is," Nancy said, setting the coin on the table. "Maybe it's toy money, like for a board game?"

"And what is that a picture of, anyway?" Bess said, pointing to the image on the coin. "A bus? A train? A space shuttle? George, what do you think?"

But George didn't respond. She was staring out the window.

Bess tapped on her shoulder. "Um, George? A little help here? We have a mystery to solve!"

George turned around. Her brown eyes were sparkling. "I think I just did!" she said excitedly.

CHAPTER EIGHT

Family Tree

"What do you mean you solved the mystery?" Nancy said curiously.

"Well, I didn't solve the *whole* mystery," George replied. "But I think I know what the picture on the gold coin is."

She pointed out the window of the restaurant. A blue-and-gold trolley car was rolling to a stop outside.

Then George pointed to the gold coin. "This isn't a picture of a bus or a train or a space shuttle. It's a picture of a trolley!" she announced.

"Oh, wow, you're right!" Bess cried out.

Hannah returned to the table, tucking

her wallet into her purse. "What's all the excitement, girls? What did I miss?"

"Remember the gold coin we found outside Rowena's cottage?" Nancy said. "George just figured out what the picture on it is. It's a trolley!"

Hannah bent down and squinted at the coin. "George is absolutely right! Which means that this coin is probably a trolley token."

Bess frowned. "A . . . what?"

"A trolley token. Some trolleys take tokens instead of money," Hannah explained. "Of course, these days, it's usually—"

Nancy jumped to her feet, not waiting for the rest of Hannah's sentence. "I'll be right back!" she announced. She grabbed the trolley token from the table and raced out to the sidewalk. The blue-and-gold trolley was still parked on the street as riders got on and off.

Nancy went up to the driver. He had a bushy white beard and tiny wire-rimmed glasses. Out of the corner of her eye she saw George, Bess, and Hannah running out of the Seashell Café to catch up to her.

"Excuse me, sir. Is this a trolley token?" Nancy asked the driver breathlessly. She held up the gold coin for him to see.

The driver bent down to take a closer look. "Well, yes, this *is* a trolley token," he said after a moment.

Nancy grinned. "Yay!"

"But hold up, young lady. This is a very old token. We haven't used tokens like these in at least fifty years—not since I used to ride this trolley as a young boy," the driver went on.

Nancy's face fell. "Oh."

"No, missy, you're not likely to see these around Cape Mermaid anymore. They're historical relics," the driver continued. "But if you want to ride the trolley now, kids are free, as long as they're with a—"

"Historical relics?" Nancy cut in. She turned to George, Bess, and Hannah. "We've got to get over to the history museum right away!" she said.

"Why are we here?" George asked Nancy when they reached the front door of the Cape Mermaid History Museum.

"I know! I wasn't done with my blueberry pancakes yet," Bess complained.

Nancy held up the trolley token. "The driver said this is a historical relic. The history museum is full of historical relics, right? So maybe Mrs. Bishop can help us figure out where this came from."

"Oh, I get it! And whoever the token belonged to may have dropped it by accident outside of Rowena's cottage yesterday," Bess said. "Nancy, you're a genius!"

Nancy beamed. "Thanks, Bess!"

The four of them headed into the museum. Mrs. Bishop was at the front desk, poring over a catalog.

She glanced up and frowned. "You're Tessie Katz's friends, aren't you? Are you here to ask me more questions about your so-called ghost?" she said irritably.

But before Nancy or her friends could answer, a man entered the lobby from an adjoining room. "Rowena, I need to get your signature on this contract." He stopped when he saw the girls. "Oh, I'm so sorry, you're in the middle of something."

Nancy's eyes widened.

Did the man just call Mrs. Bishop "Rowena"?

And then she remembered the "Family Tree" section of Rowena Ellison's biography. According to it, Mrs. Ellison had three daughters. One of those daughters had named her own daughter Rowena.

"Are you Rowena Ellison's granddaughter?" Nancy asked Mrs. Bishop. "Is that why you've been pretending to be her ghost?"

CHAPTER NINE

An Almost Invisible Clue

Mrs. Bishop stared at Nancy. "W-what did you say?" she said in a trembling voice.

"Are you Mrs. Ellison's granddaughter?" Nancy repeated.

Mrs. Bishop turned to the man. "Franklin, I'll look over that contract later. Can you give us a moment?" she asked him.

"Yes, of course." Franklin nodded and exited the lobby.

Bess, George, and Hannah were all looking at Nancy with surprised expressions.

"How did you know?" Bess asked Nancy.

"Rowena isn't a supercommon name," Nancy explained. "Plus, I read in Mrs. Ellison's biography that she had a granddaughter named Rowena."

Mrs. Bishop was silent for a moment.

"Okay, yes, Rowena Ellison was my grandmother," she admitted finally. "But I don't know anything about this ghost business!" she declared.

Nancy pulled the trolley token out of her pocket and showed it to Mrs. Bishop. "Is this yours?"

Mrs. Bishop gasped. "Oh my goodness, where did you find this? I've been looking all over for it! We're in the process of setting up a new transportation exhibit. I was carrying this trolley token around with me yesterday because I was going to take it over to the frame shop to have it mounted. But then it disappeared!"

"We found it just outside of your grandma's

cottage," Bess spoke up. "You must have dropped it there yesterday—"

"—when you were pretending to be her ghost. You really, really scared Michaela and Emma!" George spoke up.

"No, no, that's all wrong!" Mrs. Bishop said, holding up her hands. "I mean, yes, I was at the cottage. But I wasn't pretending to be a ghost. You see, I'm trying to raise money to have my grandmother's cottage fixed up and returned to its original condition. You saw what it was like. It's very run-down. The cottage is an important part of Cape Mermaid history because of who my grandmother was. It should be restored, and there should be a placard—a sign—in front, telling visitors all about it and about her work as an artist." She added, "I was at the cottage yesterday making a list of everything that has to be done to fix it up."

Nancy considered this. "So you weren't trying to scare Michaela and Emma?"

"Absolutely not! I saw those girls peeking through the front window, and the next thing I knew, they screamed their heads off and ran away," Mrs. Bishop explained.

Nancy realized that Michaela and Emma must have seen Mrs. Bishop through the window and thought she was a ghost. That made sense.

She remembered that Mrs. Bishop was wearing white yesterday. With her long gray hair, she could have looked a little ghostly, especially through a dirty, hard-to-see-through window.

But George had more questions for Mrs. Bishop.

"Were you in the attic of the Mermaid Inn on Monday night, making spooky noises and writing a spooky message?" she said. "And have you been haunting the Cape Mermaid Public Library, too?"

"Haunting the library? My goodness, no. And no, I wasn't in the attic of the Mermaid

Inn doing anything *spooky*." Mrs. Bishop sighed and shook her head. "I don't know what this ghost nonsense is about. But I would really like you girls to stop spreading stories about my grandmother's so-called ghost haunting the four corners of Cape Mermaid. It's been hurting my efforts to raise money for her cottage. Come, I'll show you."

She gestured for Nancy, George, Bess, and Hannah to follow her into the Coral Room.

She stopped in front of the Rowena Ellison exhibit and pointed to the photograph of the cottage.

"See how beautiful it used to be?" she said brightly. "It was built by her husband as a wedding present for her. She used the cottage mostly as an artist's studio. On rainy days she would paint inside. On sunny days she would paint outside, looking out toward the sea. She was most famous for her seascapes."

Nancy turned her gaze to Rowena Ellison's sea paintings, which were mounted side by side on the wall. Then she noticed something she hadn't seen before: Rowena Ellison's tiny signature, in the lower right-hand corner of each of her paintings.

Nancy leaned forward and studied the signatures intently.

The handwriting *looked* like the handwriting of the *HELP ME* message in the attic. The letters were kind of block-y, and the two *Ls* in Ellison that were in caps were just like the letter *L* in the word *HELP* had been.

"Hannah, do you have your digital camera with you?" Nancy asked her suddenly.

Hannah dug into her purse. "Yes, of course."

"Can I borrow it? I need to take a picture," Nancy replied.

Hannah handed the camera to Nancy. "A picture of what?"

"Of this." Nancy pointed to Rowena Ellison's signature. She took the camera and pressed various buttons. She zoomed in on the signature and clicked away.

"Kids and their technology," Hannah said to Mrs. Bishop with a chuckle. "She knows how to use that camera better than I do!"

MICHAELA: Do I have chocolate on my face?

EMMA: No, silly! Hey, Tessie, is the camera on?

TESSIE: Yes, it's on! Guys, come on, I'm ready to start!

EMMA: Okay, okay! You don't have to be so *mean* about it!

It was Wednesday night. Nancy, George, Bess, Tessie, Michaela, and Emma were gathered around Tessie's computer, watching the video footage of the ghost mystery so far. Tessie had a bunch of separate clips, from several weeks ago to now. This one was from the previous afternoon.

TESSIE: Michaela and Emma, you saw Rowena's ghost staring at you through the window of her cottage. Please tell us in your own words . . . what did she look like? Did she say anything to you?

MICHAELA: She was superscary.

EMMA: Yeah, super-superscary!

Nancy spoke up. "Hey, Tessie? This is interesting, but . . . could you rewind or fast-forward or whatever to the stuff from Monday night? I want to compare the handwriting on the wall to Rowena's signature from her paintings."

"Sure!" Tessie pressed the rewind button. A few seconds later she hit the pause button. The screen froze on the image of the words *HELP ME* scrawled on the dusty attic wall.

Nancy scrolled through the photos on

Hannah's camera and found the ones she'd taken at the museum that afternoon of Rowena Ellison's signature. Then she gazed at the computer screen. The handwriting *did* look similar.

Tessie peered over Nancy's shoulder. "They look exactly the same! See? That's proof that Rowena Ellison's ghost really exists. Right, guys?" She elbowed Michaela and Emma, who were sitting on either side of her.

"Right!" Michaela and Emma said in unison.

"But what about what Mrs. Bishop said?" George piped up. "She said there *is* no ghost of her grandmother."

"Well, she's wrong," Tessie insisted. "Hey, you guys want to see my interviews of Mrs. Yamada?" she added brightly.

While Tessie pressed the fast-forward button, Nancy pulled the mermaid notebook out of her backpack and began flipping through the pages. She wanted to find the entry about the "Help me" message and read what she'd written.

But Nancy accidentally turned too many

pages at once and landed on a blank one. She started to turn back when she noticed something odd.

There were faint, almost invisible marks all over this particular page. They looked like impressions or indentations from someone's writing on the *previous* page.

But that page had been ripped out.

Nancy curled the notebook over so she could see just that single page against the light. Squinting, she could make out a single phrase, written over and over again:

Help me
Help me
Help me
Help me
Help me
Help me

Nancy whirled around to Michaela. "*You're* the ghost!" she cried out.

Chapter Ten

The Competition

Michaela began twirling a lock of her hair around and around her index finger. "Ha-ha, that's superfunny," she said nervously.

"Nancy, what are you talking about?" George asked her.

Nancy held the notebook page up to the light so that everyone could see. "Someone wrote the words 'Help me' over and over again on the page *before* this one, like they were trying to copy Rowena's handwriting," she said, pointing. "It had to be Michaela. She gave me this notebook yesterday. She tore some pages out first, though."

Bess put her hands on her hips. "Michaela, that's *awful*!" she cried out. "Why have you been pretending to be Rowena's ghost?"

Michaela looked away. "I *didn't*! I mean, I *kind* of did, but it's only because Tessie said—"

"Michaela, be *quiet*!" Tessie ordered her.

"Tessie said what?" Nancy asked Michaela.

"Tessie, we *have* to tell them the truth," Emma spoke up.

Tessie frowned at Emma and Michaela. Then she let out a heavy sigh. "Oh . . . *fine*," she said finally.

Tessie opened her desk drawer and pulled out a piece of light green paper. She slid it across the desk toward Nancy, George, and Bess.

Nancy looked over it quickly. It was a flyer for a contest. It said:

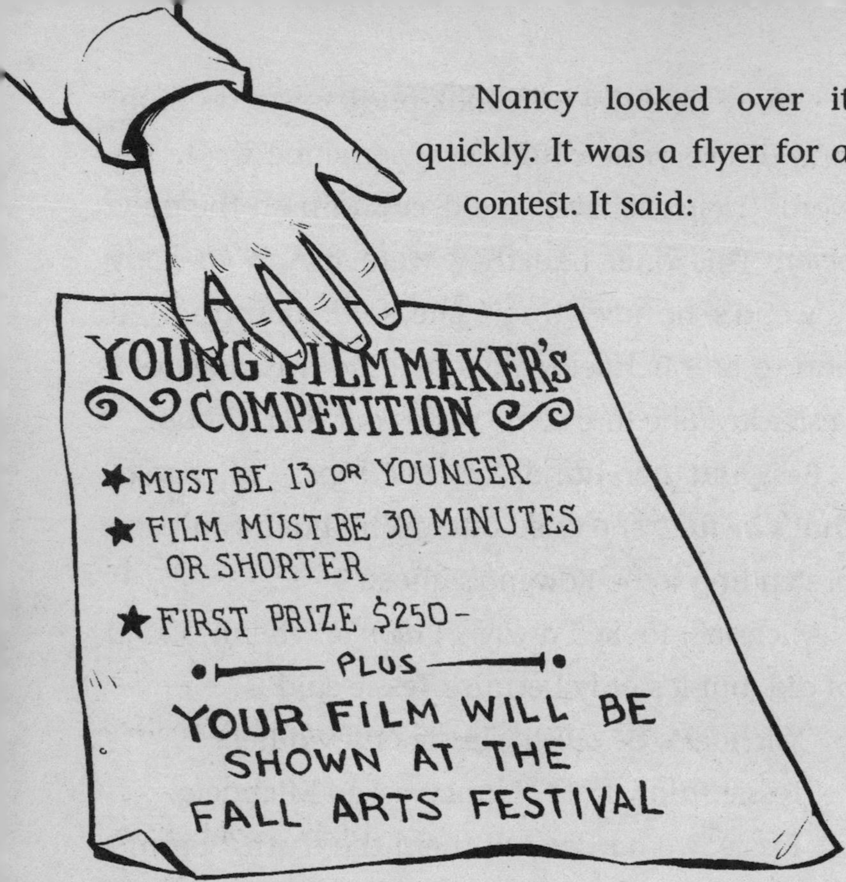

YOUNG FILMMAKER'S COMPETITION

* MUST BE 13 OR YOUNGER
* FILM MUST BE 30 MINUTES OR SHORTER
* FIRST PRIZE $250 -

PLUS

YOUR FILM WILL BE SHOWN AT THE FALL ARTS FESTIVAL

Nancy glanced up. "A filmmaker's competition?"

Tessie nodded, her blue eyes shining. "Yup! As soon as I saw this, I knew we had to enter the competition! I even came up with this awesome idea to make a short documentary about Rowena Ellison's ghost and how she was haunting Cape Mermaid."

"The problem was, there *was* no ghost. And a documentary is supposed to be a movie about the truth, about stuff that really happened," Emma piped up. "So we decided to make up a ghost and pretend she was real."

"We saw the Rowena Ellison exhibit at the history museum on a school field trip last spring," Michaela explained. "We thought Rowena would make a supercool ghost."

"Soooooo . . . the noises in the attic on Monday night? And the message on the wall?" Bess asked the three girls.

"We came up with that plan right after spaghetti and meatballs," Emma said sheepishly. "Later, after Michaela and I said good-bye to you guys and left Tessie's room, we went up to the attic and, you know, did our ghost thing."

"We snuck back down the other stairs—the back stairs—and left through the kitchen,"

Michaela continued. "No one saw us. And you were right, Nancy. I wrote the words 'Help me' on the wall. I practiced Rowena's handwriting over and over again."

Nancy considered all this. "What about the video you recorded at Rowena's cottage two weeks ago? How did you fake that?" she asked Tessie.

"Easy! We found some shimmery white cloth in the attic," Tessie replied. "We took it out to Rowena's cottage one day. Emma held it up with a stick and Michaela shined a flashlight through it. The wind was kind of blowing it around too. It really looked like a ghost!"

"It really did!" Bess agreed.

"What about Mrs. Yamada's stories?" George said. "Was she helping you guys pretend about Rowena's ghost?"

Tessie shook her head. "No way! She heard we were making a movie about the ghost, and she told us all that stuff. My mom always said Mrs. Yamada is very, um, imaginative."

"Yeah. Last year, Mrs. Yamada thought she saw a unicorn in the woods near the beach," Michaela said, giggling.

Nancy was silent for a moment. "Okay, so, now we know the whole truth," she said finally. "Still, it wasn't very nice of you guys to lie to us before."

"I know, and I'm so, so sorry!" Tessie apologized. "It's just that . . . well . . . we were so psyched when you guys showed up and said you had a detective club called the Clue Crew. We thought that would make our movie even better if you tried to find Rowena's 'ghost.'"

"I'm sorry too!" Michaela said.

"I'm sorry three!" Emma added. "If we take you out for ice cream tomorrow, will you forgive us?"

"Yes!" Bess said, raising her hand.

Everyone laughed.

On the last night of their vacation in Cape Mermaid, Nancy pulled out her mermaid notebook and wrote:

Well, everyone knows the truth now. There is no ghost of Rowena Ellison.

Tessie, Michaela, and Emma told their parents, Mrs. Bishop, Mrs. Yamada, and lots of other people the whole story. Plus, they said they were sorry.

I think Tessie's parents said she can't watch TV or use her computer for the rest of the month because of what she did. (I think Michaela's and Emma's parents said the same thing.)

Tessie's parents also said that the girls should make a new movie, about Rowena

Ellison and her cottage and how it needs to be fixed up. Tessie thought that was a great idea, so that's what they're going to do.

Tessie said that if they win the movie contest, they're going to give the prize money to Mrs. Bishop so she can use it for fixing up the cottage.

Mystery solved!

P.S. We're driving back to River Heights tomorrow. I'll be able to use my purple detective notebook again! I mean, you're pretty cool, mermaid notebook. But I kind of miss my old one!

P.P.S. I wonder if there will be a new mystery waiting for us when we get home????

GET YOUR FEET READY FOR SUMMER WITH SOME FFFF's (FANCY, FLUFFY FLIP-FLOPS!)

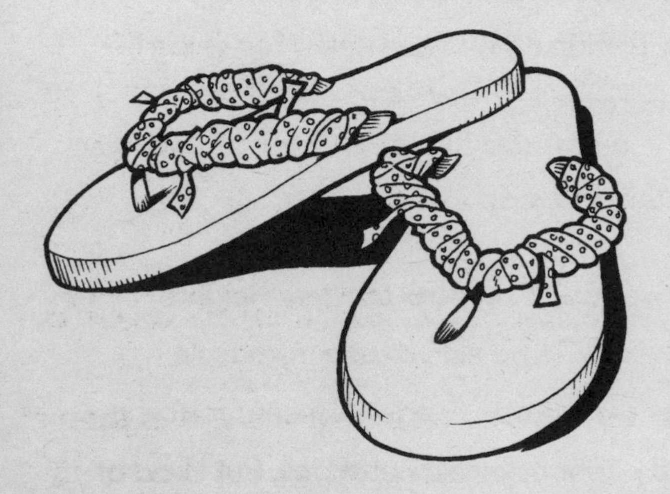

Nancy, George, and Bess love to wear fancy, fluffy flip-flops to the beach or pool. You can make your own in just minutes with this simple do-it-yourself craft!

YOU WILL NEED:

A pair of flip-flops

Scissors

Pretty fabric and/or cloth ribbon.*

*NOTE: The ribbon should be about one inch wide. You'll need enough fabric or ribbon to make about twenty to thirty one-inch-by-eight-inch strips (See Step #1, below). You can choose a single color to match your flip-flops (like baby blue), or you can use lots of different colors and patterns. Go crazy!

THEN FOLLOW THESE EASY STEPS:

- Cut the fabric into one-inch-by-eight-inch strips. If you're using ribbon, cut it into eight-inch strips. If your scissors are supersharp, make sure to ask your parents for help!
- Aim for about twenty to thirty strips. The more strips you have, the fluffier your flip-flops will be!
- Tie the strips around the flip-flop straps. Use single knots, not bows.
- Push the knots close together as you go. Stop

when your flip-flops are at their maximum fluffiness!

- ❀ OPTIONAL: For a different kind of fancy flip-flops, you could get some cute buttons or colorful feathers at a craft store and glue them onto your flip-flop straps with white glue.

THEN STEP IN TO YOUR SWANKY NEW SHOES AND ENJOY THE SUN, SAND, AND SURF IN STYLE!

Candy Fairies

Read all the books in the Candy Fairies series!

Visit candyfairies.com for more delicious fun with your favorite fairies.

Play games, download activities, and so much more!

From Aladdin
PUBLISHED BY SIMON & SCHUSTER